Eli and Mort's Epic Adventure
Beaver Creek

2015 World Championship Special Edition

About this project

The idea for the Eli and Mort adventure series came from the joy we experienced watching our kids ski, snowboard and have the time of their lives growing up in the Vail Valley. We wanted to share that joy and this beautiful place with the world. We decided to write a book about the Vail Valley through the eyes of a child on a vacation adventure.

When considering the concept we imagined what a child might see and feel when they stood at the top of the mountain about to take the first run of the day, and thought, "Who better qualified to illustrate the book than the children that live here?" As a result, we agreed the background illustrations should be drawn by the children of the Vail Valley.

About the characters

Eli and his pal Mort the moose are the best of friends exploring the world together. In this book, they are experiencing not only the Vail Valley, but the 2015 FIS World Ski Championships taking place in Beaver Creek.

Eli and Mort are dedicated to the loves of our lives,
Josh, Heath & Will.

Enjoy!

Created by Elyssa Pallai and Ken Nager
Published by ResortBooks
Background illustrations by the children of the Vail Valley
Background cover illustration by: Anabel Johnson
Character illustrations by Eduardo Paj

Production Date: September 2014
Plant & Location: Printed by We SP Corp., Seoul, Korea
Job/Batch# 42517-0/WESP-140805

Thank you

We love our friends in the Vail Valley. Mort and I think you are AWESOME! Special thanks to Eduardo Paj for making us look so good, Nicole Magistro from the Bookworm who inspired us to write this, Lauren Merrill at Alpine Arts Center, Brent Bingham and PhotoFX, Jen Bruno from Luca Bruno for her retail advice, Chris Mitchell for her creative input and Brenda Himelfarb for making sure what we wrote was what we meant to write. Hooray to all of the AWESOME parents of the kids that illustrated this book and the Vail Valley Foundation and Youth Foundation for their ongoing support in helping us reach the world.

Visit **resortbooks.net** to order our latest adventure, see where we are on with our "Eli and Mort Adventure Tracker," or to just say, "Hi!"

YOUTH FOUNDATION
Vail Valley Foundation's Education Arm

A portion of the proceeds of this book go to the Youth Foundation.

The Illustrators

Eli and Mort would like to thank the AMAZING children that illustrated the backgrounds — ages 7 to 17! Below are some of their favorite things to do in Beaver Creek. What's yours?

D
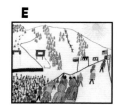

Adeline
Eagle County Charter School
10 years old
Favorite: Ski Jack Rabbit Alley and then eat chocolate chip cookies

I

Annika Dupont
Vail Mountain School
13 years old
Favorite: I love to ice skate

E
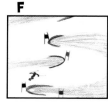

AnaBel Johnson
Battle Mountain High School
15 years old
Favorite: Eat cookies and ski

J

Tommy Johnson
Berry Creek Middle School
11 years old
Favorite: Ski

A

Caleb Dennis
Homestake Peak School
13 years old
Favorite: Back country skiing

F

Lauren ElizaBeth Rumley
Home schooled
10 years old
Favorite: Going down the tubing hill and bungee jumping

K

Eva Thomas
Vail Mountain School
10 years old
Favorite: Ice skating and skiing Jack Rabbit Alley

B
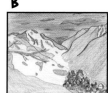

Hannah Litt
Eagle County Charter School
12 years old
Favorite: Performing at the Vilar Center

G
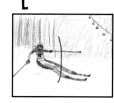

Leah Ratchford
Eagle Valley Middle School
11 years old
Favorite: Ski the tree runs in winter and hike in the summer

L
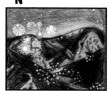

Mika Leith
Homestake Peak School
12 years old
Favorite: Running the Eric Spry Memorial Race

C

Kendra Louise Hoyt
Vail Ski & Snowboard Academy
14 years old
Favorite: Eat chocolate chip cookies and ski

H

Addison Mauer
Berry Creek Middle School
10 years old
Favorite: Ski and tubing

N

Ella Smiley
Brush Creek Elementary
7 years old
Favorite: Eat the free chocolate chip cookies after skiing

O

Willa Healey

Homestake Peak School
11 years old
Favorite: Ski with my family on Sundays

P

Grace ChristenBerry

Berry Creek Middle School
11 years old
Favorite: Ski with my friends down Royal Elk Glade

Q

Annie Cooper

Vail Mountain School
11 years old
Favorite: Ice Skating

R

Sophie Russell

Berry Creek Middle School
11 years old
Favorite: Ski

S

Alessandro Cantele

Edwards Elementary School
10 years old
Favorite: Ski fresh corduroy right behind a snowcat

T

Lorenzo Molinar

Berry Creek Middle School
11 years old
Favorite: Snowboard and explore Beaver Creek Village

U

Dylan Berlin Dodds

Stone Creek Charter School
10 years old
Favorite: Ski and perform the Nutcracker at the Vilar Center during the Christmas season

V

Taylor Petersen

Battle Mountain High School
17 years old
Favorite: Ski with Dad

W

Malia Braden

Gypsum Creek Middle School
11 years old
Favorite: Loves to ski

X

Grant Mauer

Berry Creek Middle School
12 years old
Favorite: Ski and snowboard

Y

Montana Braden

Gypsum Creek Middle School
13 years old
Favorite: Lives to snowboard (In fact, she races snowboards!)

Z

Taylor Louise Hoyt

Eagle County Charter Academy
11 years old
Favorite: Eat cookies and ski

A is for Airplane that I flew in with my stepmom, Dad, Lil' Sis, Mort my moose, and the marshmallows now squished in my pocket that I was saving. I took the marshmallows with me because I thought Mort might get hungry on his first plane trip, and because I wanted to see if the color of the marshmallows matched the snow.

We came here especially to see the 2015 World Ski Championships. Mort can't wait for this adventure. Neither can I!

B is for Beaver Creek. As we arrived, my dad said we weren't roughing it. I thought to myself, "I like roughing it and so does Mort." I wasn't sure what he meant by, "not roughing it," until I saw the view outside my window. Being in Beaver Creek wasn't roughing it at all. It was a beautiful mountain village. Mort thought so too.

Hannah Litt

C is for Chocolate Chip Cookies. My stepmom told me that they served cookies at the bottom of the mountain at three o'clock, so off we went. As we ran through the snow, Mort and I thought about hot chocolate chips mushing and smooshing between our teeth. Mort took extra ones and put them in my pocket. The melty chips stuck to his fur. He needed a bath.

D is for Downhill race on the Birds of Prey downhill course where most of the 2015 races take place. For practice I decided to race my stepmom while my dad timed us. All I cared about was beating Lil' Sis down the hill, so Mort and I practiced all day.

E is for Everyone. There were over 700 athletes from 70 nations taking part in the Championships. All the different skiers from different countries were here with their flags held high. I liked the American Flag the best. So did Mort.

F is for FUN! Mort and I had so much fun watching the men's slalom I had to try it. I read in a book that if you imagine yourself doing something, you can do it. I spent the afternoon imagining Mort and me doing the slalom. Swoosh, swoosh swoosh. I only touched one flag. Mort touched two.

G is for Gondola. Beaver Creek built a brand new combination lift with gondolas and chairs. I rode it with my stepmom and Mort on my way to watch the racers fly down the mountain. The person that let my stepmom, Mort and me on the lift told us that it can carry 3,400 people an hour up the mountain. How much is 3,400? I wasn't sure. Either was Mort. But it's A LOT!

Leah R

H is for Haymaker Tubing Hill. My dad says it is the perfect family-friendly adventure area for winter fun. I wasn't sure what he meant but nodded anyway. As we flew down the hill, Mort was screaming his head off and laughing all at once. My lil' sis was embarrassed. But, she's usually the one screaming.

I is for Ice Skating. My lil' sis thought the ice rink was so romantic. (Romantic stuff is yucky!) As we skated we caught snowflakes on our tongues and mittens. My sis thought they looked like little pieces of white lace. Mort loved to eat them. I liked to watch them disappear into my mitten.

J is for Jack Rabbit Alley, my favorite ski run. It was swoopy and flowy and just hard enough for Mort and me. It also had some cool signs on it that talked about different animals on the mountain. Now Mort and I know what a squirrel print looks like in the snow. Do you know what a squirrel print looks like?

K is for Kids Adventure Zone where I learned to do tons of cool tricks, including skiing through a teepee. I sat underneath the teepee for a couple of minutes wondering what life was like in one. Then I decided to do some jumps. They were REALLY big. Mort thought that was cool and asked me to do them over and again. So I did.

EvX

MIKA LEITH

L is for Ladies Super G. Mort and I shouted, "WOW!" as we watched the skiers fly past. My dad says that the racers ski down the mountain at over 70 miles an hour. I had a hard time thinking about skiers going faster than our car. I thought my dad was fast. But that was REALLY fast.

M is for Mort the moose OF COURSE! Pete the Mountain Lion and Earl the Raccoon are Mort's new friends. We took the Cinch Express up to Park 101, the terrain park at Beaver Creek, where we "caught huge air" and "crushed it." Those are the new words for skiing and jumping that Mort learned from Pete and Earl. We had a blast. So did Pete and Earl.

N is for Night sky. "Whoa," Mort said. I said, "Whoa," too as we looked up. I had never seen so many stars all at once. I squinted and un-squinted over and again making the stars look like fireworks. My stepmom told me to stop because my eyes might freeze that way. I believed her. So did Mort.

is for Opening Ceremonies at Championships Plaza. The National Anthem was my favorite part. Mort and I stood pretending we were in the middle of the stage singing it. I opened my mouth wide and sang as loud as I could. Singing loud made me feel warm on the inside. I knew every word. So did Mort.

P is for Powder Day. We woke up to an, "EPIC powder day."

"Powder" I learned is soft snow. I could tell having a epic powder day made my dad happy. Skiing the powder was like floating on a cloud. The snow was so deep I thought Mort could not breathe while he was skiing. But, he was fine because he had his snorkel with him.

2014 Grace

Q is for high-speed Quad. My favorite was riding the Rose Bowl High Speed Quad. You could see for miles and miles AND miles. Mort liked chair Eight, the Cinch Express because it took us to Park 101 where we had freeskied with Pete and Earl going over jumps and rails. That Rocked!

Annie Cooper

R is for Restaurants. There were so many to choose from but Mort's favorite was OBVIOUSLY the Blue Moose. He liked the moose and Mort's favorite food is pizza. So is mine. The Blue Moose has the best pizza in Beaver Creek. That's our opinion. What's yours?

Alessandro C.

S is for Snowcat. It was fun to watch the gigantic machines smooth out the moguls on the mountain. They made it easier for us to ski down the slope. Moguls were tough, but so was Mort. Snowcats flattened moguls and turned them into corduroy, so it looked like flat snow with wavy marks in it. I thought that was AWESOME. So did Mort.

T is for Trails. Beaver Creek has 150 trails. I don't think
     Mort and I skied that many trails during the whole
week we were there. Maybe twenty one or twenty two. Not 150. How
many is 150? Anyway, we saw a red fox at the bottom of the mountain.
I asked Mort, "What does a fox say?" Mort wasn't sure.

U is for Up top of the mountain. We were REALLY, REALLY, REALLY high. I think we could see for a bazillion miles. "Whoopie! Let's rip it up," I yelled. And down we went. Beaver Creek ROCKS!

Dylan Dodds

V is for Vilar Performing Arts Center. My stepmom loved getting dressed up to see a show at night. My sis loved it too. Mort and I didn't like the dress up part, or the sitting still part, but we did our best for her. The Vilar Center was a really cool place to see a show.

W is for Wedge. My lil' sis learned how to turn without using a wedge. She got so much better after we skied a few days. She still couldn't beat Mort and me though.

Brant W Maurer

X is for the eXpert ski patrol that kept the mountain safe. They wore bright red jackets so they were easy to find. Mort and I asked them about how to be safe on the mountain. They were super nice and told us things like how it's important not to go too fast. They said, "Hello Eli!" as I skied by.

Y is for Yelling, "whoo hoo!" as my lil' sis beat my stepmom through the race flags. Either we kept getting faster, or my stepmom kept getting slower. I wasn't sure which one. Neither was Mort. But either way, my sis was happy.

Z is for the racers Zooming down the hill. I tried hard to keep my eyes on them as they flew past. So did Mort. I hope one day I can ski as fast as they did. I loved watching the 2015 Championships. So did Mort and my lil' sis. And she's not easy to please. We can't wait until our next adventure!

T. Hoyt

Autographs

Eli

Mort